The REINDEER'S SHOE
AND OTHER STORIES
BY
KARLE WILSON BAKER

Illustrated by Charlotte Baker

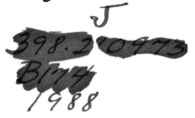

[E]LLEN C. TEMPLE
AUSTIN, TEXAS

WITH

STEPHEN F. AUSTIN STATE UNIVERSITY
NACOGDOCHES, TEXAS

Library of Congress Cataloging-in-Publication Data

Baker, Karle Wilson, 1878-1960.
    The reindeer's shoe and other stories.

    Contents: The reindeer's shoe—The Storm King's plume—The reaching
princess—[etc.]
    1. Fairy tales—United States. 2. Children's stories, American. [1. Fairy
tales. 2. Short stories]
I. Baker, Charlotte, 1910-   ill. II. Title.
PZ8.B174Re 1988   [E]   88-2292
ISBN 0-936650-07-9

First Edition

Printed in the United States of America

Text and cover design by Charlotte Baker Montgomery.

Production by Dodson Publication Services, Austin, Texas

NOTES: The illustrations in this book are reproductions of the original cut-
        paper silhouettes.

        Pamela Lynn Palmer, Stephen F. Austin State University, who
        contributed the biographical sketch, is currently working on a full-
        length biography about the life of Karle Wilson Baker.

        Francis E. Abernethy, Stephen F. Austin State University,
        served as coeditor for this book.

Ellen C. Temple, Publisher
1011 Westlake Drive, Suite #900
Austin, TX 78746

CONTENTS

TO THE READER

These stories, written by my mother some sixty years ago, are now in print for the first time. Just think! During all those years children never had a chance to read how Gleam, the reindeer, found his lost shoe; whether the princess ever got what she was reaching for; what the crow told the king's forester's son; and who came to visit the little old lady on the mountain when the wild geese began to fly south. Somehow the calendar must have stuck, like the ones that stuck Three-Weeks-Before-Christmas when Gleam lost his little silver shoe.

In another book, my mother once wrote, "When I was a little girl, I used to go inside my head and play." Her mind was a magical playground for her imagination. There the things she cared about were turned into stories, novels, essays, and poetry. Trees and people and weather and birds and family and far-away places and courage and skies and butterflies and perfection and home—these are some of the things you can find in her books.

My brother and I were lucky to grow up in a house full of books. Our parents read aloud to us, and very soon we could read for ourselves. I always asked for books for Christmas and birthdays. Looking forward to a new book added to the fun of it. More so because I received it the night before the great day and slept with it, gift-wrap and all. No time was lost opening it next morning.

The books I liked best had pictures. The best pictures were like windows opening right into the story. It seemed to me that a book with pictures like that was just about the finest thing in the world.

When the publication of *The Reindeer's Shoe and Other Stories* was being planned, the question of illustrations came up at once. All concerned wanted the pictures to be just right. That is, they must *belong* in the book. We thought that such pictures might be hard to find.

Then I recalled that I had once tried to illustrate these stories myself, at least fifty years ago. As far as I could remember, I had worked very hard, without success, and finally had bundled up the sketches and put them away.

I found them in my filing cabinet. Many were failures and many were unfinished. But there was one set of cut-paper silhouettes, completed, matted and labeled, ready for use. Evidently my mother and I had liked them and thought they belonged in the book.

We hope you will agree. And now that the calendar has come unstuck, we invite you to read the stories and make up for lost time.

CHARLOTTE BAKER

6

THE REINDEER'S SHOE

G leam, one of Saint Nicholas' reindeer, had lost one of his silver shoes. Going home with a load of crystals late one frosty evening, just as the stars were coming out, he had nicked it against the tallest spire of the City on the Island. Down it had gone, tinkling and twinkling, until it was lost somewhere among the streets of the city.

The misfortune was serious, for Christmas could not come until the reindeer found his shoe. Saint Nicholas, though so jolly, is careful and humane. How could he drive his team on that long, swift journey over the frozen sky, if one of the reindeer were lame from a missing shoe? So all the calendars in the world stuck tight at Three-Weeks-Before Christmas. All the grown people, being busy with less important things, thought that they were ticking along as usual. But Saint Nicholas was very uneasy, for the children were beginning to suspect.

The island on which the city was situated was high and rocky, and set in the midst of a bright green sea. And the city itself was the tallest in the world. The shops and castles and churches climbed one above the other up the steep streets, and on the evening when the shoe was lost, there was snow all over the housetops, and the lights were beginning to shine out over the green sea.

Stocking, who was driving the reindeer team, was very much put out when he saw what had happened. He was Saint Nicholas' trusted helper, and he felt that he had been to blame for driving so low in his hurry. He leaned over the side of his sleigh and watched the faint, silver twinkle as the shoe fell down, down, down. At last he lost sight of it between the snowy roof tops. Stocking was a slim, graceful elf who always dressed in black silk jersey-cloth, with a jaunty little pointed cap of black. Usually he was as gay and brisk a little fellow as ever slipped down a chimney. Now he was crest-fallen and sorrowful as he gathered up the reins.

There was great dismay in Saint Nicholas' castle when the loss was known. It was perfectly clear that all the calendars in the world had already stuck tight at Three-Weeks-Before-Christmas, and none knew better than Saint Nicholas how quick children are to notice that time is not going as it should. Stocking made a full report of the incident, not attempting to excuse himself at all, and it was presently arranged that he should ride Gleam, and go in search of the lost shoe.

There were two things only that he was cautioned not to do. When he found the silver shoe, he was not to pick it up while anyone was looking, and he was not to go inside any walls for it. The reason was, that to do either was against The Nature of Things.

So Stocking and Gleam set out on their search and soon came to the spire where Gleam had lost his shoe. As they looked downward, a little boy named Timmy came whistling along the street. Timmy was not more than seven, and he was ragged and dirty, but he had a splendid wide smile with a gap in it where two teeth were missing. You would have thought Timmy must be proud of this gap, he showed it so often.

Stocking knew him very well and his heart gave a bound of relief

when he saw the lad coming, for there on the pavement, directly in his path, lay the reindeer's shoe. He would rather have it fall into Timmy's hands than into those of any mortal he knew. Timmy was such a friendly, obliging person that it would surely be easy to find a way to get the shoe back from him.

But just as Timmy's sharp eyes caught sight of it, and just as he was about to make a dive for it with his little brown paw outstretched, an old shopkeeper with a long grey beard turned into the street from an alleyway, and saw before him on the sidewalk the silver shoe. Quick as a flash he stooped and snatched it up. Then he gave Timmy such a scowl that Timmy was glad to get out of his way.

As for the old shopkeeper, he stood still with the silver shoe in his palm, stroking his beard with the other hand, and wetting his sly lips with the tip of his tongue. He saw at once that this was a priceless thing. To be sure, it was only of silver, but it was chased all over with fairy designs like frost-work. It gave forth of itself a silvery radiance which told the beholder at once that it was altogether out of the ordinary. And the nails—all but one of which were still sticking in the nail-holes—were of diamonds.

While the old man stood looking at it in amazement, Stocking and Gleam came swooping down upon him from the cold stars. He gave a startled look around, for they came so suddenly that he heard the jingling of Gleam's bells. He thought it was a gust of wind from around the corner, clinking the icicles on the sign that creaked over his door. Nevertheless, he thrust the jewel—for such he thought it—into his bosom under his cloak. He turned his collar up about his ears, hastily unlocked the door of his shop and went in. Then he locked the door behind him, leaving the unhappy Stocking and Gleam outside.

Presently a light shone through a crack in the shutter. Stocking crept up and looked in. He could get a glimpse of two rooms. The front room of the curiosity shop, where customers were received, was poor and mean. There was nothing much in it but old musical instruments and picture frames, and a few rings and brooches, and big watches hung up by plated chains.

But the back room was full of wonderful things. It had rugs and tapestries that glowed in the candle light, and priceless vases of jade and agate. And in the wall it had a jewel-filled cabinet which the shopkeeper opened by a secret spring.

As Stocking watched through the crack he saw the old man take out casket after casket of jewels, comparing each jewel with the little shoe

12

of silver and diamonds. Each time he put one of the cases back he would rub his hands and moisten his lips with his tongue. Nothing he had was as fine as the silver shoe.

When he had looked at them all, he brought a jade-and-ivory box from under a pile of old stuffs in the corner where it had been cunningly hidden. He unlocked it with an ivory key, and put the reindeer's shoe in the box, folded in a velvet cloth. Then he sat down and took off his shoes, and put the little key in the toe of his sock.

And *then* the old shopkeeper put the jade-and-ivory box back into the cabinet and closed the cabinet with the secret spring and drew a plush curtain over it. He placed his big armchair plump against the curtain, sat down, folded his arms, leaned his head back against the curtain, and presently went to sleep.

All this time Stocking had been watching through the crack in the shutter. When the old man closed his eyes, Stocking felt very hopeless indeed. He turned around to see if Gleam knew how badly things were going. There stood the little reindeer, pawing mournfully, his dainty head uplifted and his eyes full of sorrow.

The sight of him made Stocking take courage. He must find a way! But nothing could be done until morning, when the shopkeeper might perhaps come outside of his walls and bring his silver jewel with him. Meantime, Stocking decided, he and Gleam must sleep.

The people of the city thought the night very cold, but Stocking and Gleam, who were used to the frosty sky-weather, found the air quite close and heavy. They looked around for a place to sleep, and decided on a church steeple nearby. There they settled themselves quite nicely. They comforted themselves by resolutions to do their best and never give up, and they slept pleasantly till morning. The only thing that disturbed them was that they could hear during the early part of the night the sighs of the children, who suspected in their dreams that the calendar had stopped.

13

The first thing they did when they awoke was to scamper off to the curiosity shop window. The old man already had his new treasure out of the cabinet and was gloating over it as it lay in his hand. Yet all the time he kept watching the door, as if he were waiting for somebody.

Before long Stocking saw a handsome coach draw up outside with the Duchess de Pomp's coat of arms on the door. The Duchess herself stepped out, covered from tip to toe with satins and velvets and laces and muffled up to her ears in the richest of furs. Between her collar and her bonnet a sharp nose stuck out, and two sharp, black eyes bored like gimlets. She spoke to her coachman in a sour and haughty voice.

The old shopkeeper backed and bowed all over his shop when he let her in. Stocking, whose ears were very keen, could hear most of the things they said.

"Five million gold pieces is a small price, madam," the shopkeeper was saying. "There has never been seen in the world a jewel like this."

"Very well," said the Duchess, taking a velvet bag from under her cloak, "I'll take it." She was clearly a person who knew what she wanted. From the minute she looked upon the silver reindeer's shoe a spark of grim triumph had glittered in her eye.

The shopkeeper looked at the bag and then at the jewel. He wetted his lips and smiled uneasily. Stocking could see that he was eager for the money, but could not bear to give up the jewel. "A small price, madam," he continued, in a soft, wheedling voice, "Far too small. Six million, now—"

"I'll give six," said the Duchess, grimly and promptly.

"Or seven," said the shopkeeper. But the words were hardly out of his mouth before the Duchess had snatched the jewel from his hand. She flung her velvet bag upon the table with a haughty gesture. Then she swept out of the room without looking around, saying as she went, "There is ten in that bag. Take it and be quiet!"

14

Stocking leaped upon Gleam's back and they dashed around to the front of the shop. If only the Duchess would drop the shoe on the pavement without missing it! But she did not. Instead, she stepped into her coach with a most triumphant expression and rode away. Gleam and Stocking could only follow to see if their chance might yet be coming.

At last the coach drove through the great gate of the next-to-the-largest palace in the city, on the next-to-the-highest hill. The largest palace on the highest hill belonged to the king and queen. But this palace was grand enough for anyone. Still, it did not seem to be a very happy place. Apparently there was no one in it but the haughty Duchess and her hundreds of servants.

The servants came running from all directions as she entered, and seemed to tremble if she looked at them. Today she paid no attention to anybody except her eighteen maids, whom she immediately ordered to begin dressing her for the Queen's Ball that night. She talked to the maids because there was nobody else in all the palace to talk to. Stocking heard what she said.

"Now at last I have something that will impress the Queen," she said. "When she sees this jewel in my hair she will desire it, for there is certainly nothing like it on the earth. And when she asks me what I will take for it, I shall say, "Make me your First Lady-in-Waiting!"

Two of the younger maids exchanged just the faintest ghost of a smile behind her back. The Duchess looked so sour and ugly when she drew herself up so proudly that she seemed more like a high-and-mighty scarecrow than a lady-in-waiting. But she seemed to feel them smiling behind her, and when she whirled around upon them they shook so that the hair-pins rattled in their hands.

All that day Gleam and Stocking hung about the next-to-the-largest palace. They saw all the eighteen maids working all day long to make the Duchess beautiful. And, indeed, by evening she was certainly

16

covered and decorated with beautiful things, the most beautiful of all being the little silver shoe that glistened in the black wig above her forehead.

The Duchess was certainly not beautiful, but it was easy to understand her air of triumph. Anyone looking at that jewel and the silvery light it shed could see that there was no other like it and that it had somehow gotten upon the earth—and the Duchess—by mistake.

That night was blue and starlit, and promptly on the hour the coach drew up at the Duchess's door, this time drawn by six silky white horses. Stocking leaned forward over Gleam's antlers, hoping that the wind would loosen the shoe from the Duchess's wig, or that she would knock it off as she entered the coach. But no, indeed! Her eighteen maids had fastened it far too securely. So Stocking could only trail along behind, wishing he had never been hasty, had never been careless—and had never let poor Gleam nick off his little shoe.

It was very easy to see in at the windows of the king's palace for they were all ablaze with lights. Stocking would have been overjoyed to watch the brilliant scene within, if his heart had not been so heavy. But even the little prince had discovered that the calendar had stopped. He sat disconsolate in a corner of the throne room, dressed in his crimson velvet, sighing. He already had everything his heart could desire, and one would not think he would care so much. Still, Christmas is Christmas, and even a prince wants Christmas when its time comes.

So Stocking, grieved to the heart, kept his eyes still more narrowly on the reindeer's shoe. The minute the Duchess de Pomp entered the room, all eyes were upon it. Even the Queen raised her beautiful tired eyes and gazed at it.

Now the Queen was the most beautiful person in the world. She was also the saddest, for she had set her heart on Something Perfect. You would have said that she was perfect herself. She was slender and white as ivory. Her hair was as pale as the new moon and her eyes as

17

green as the sea about the island. And, with it all, she was kind and sweet.

But she had a little golden mole on the back of her neck. It was hidden by a curl that seemed to escape from below her crown, but the Queen could never forget that it was there. It made her Not Perfect, and so she was always looking for something that was.

As soon as she saw the jewel in the Duchess's wig, the Queen touched the King on the arm and spoke to him a moment behind her peacock-feather fan. In a little while the King summoned the Chamberlain. Not long after that the Chamberlain sent his servant to request the Duchess to allow him a moment's conversation.

Stocking had already found a good place at the window of the Chamberlain's private audience-room when the Duchess came sweeping in.

"If you will let the Queen have the rare jewel in your hair," said the Chamberlain, after the usual formalities, "the King will give you two castles and the Queen will make you First Lady-in-Waiting."

Instantly the Duchess unfastened the reindeer's shoe from her wig and put it into the Chamberlain's hand. Then she summoned a lackey. "Tell the Second Lady-in-Waiting to present herself at once," she commanded. "And bring me a tiara—diamonds and emeralds, or rubies and pearls. Don't dawdle." And the lackey hurried off, trembling.

But Stocking and Gleam were watching the little silver shoe in the Chamberlain's hand. Surely, now, they would find some way to get it, since it was to belong to the gentle Queen!

The Chamberlain caused it to be placed upon a blue satin cushion covered with lace, and presented it to the Queen himself. "Will it please your Majesty to wear it?" he asked. "Shall I summon the Ladies-in-Waiting?"

"No," said the Queen, in a sad, sweet voice. "It is not fitting that I should wear a perfect jewel. But I will keep it by me, that I may have Something Perfect to look upon. Bring it nearer."

19

But, when they brought it, the Queen looked upon it for a moment and then suddenly swooned away. She made no sound, only a little swish of silk and lace. She would have slipped like water to the floor if the King had not caught her.

When they revived her, she would not look at the silver shoe again. She only murmured, "It is not perfect." Then the King looked closely and saw that one diamond nail was missing. Thereupon he glared at the Duchess fiercely. But the Duchess only tossed her wig and smiled. She had been made First Lady-in-Waiting, and that was all she cared about.

The ball was a grand and gay affair, in spite of the distractions caused by the reindeer's shoe. The Queen revived presently, and was able to sit beside the King on the throne, smiling sweetly and palely upon her subjects. They loved her devotedly in spite of her sadness.

As for poor Stocking and Gleam, they sadly watched the reindeer's shoe locked up for the night in the King's own jewel cabinet, which was

guarded night and day by six men-at-arms. Finding that there was nothing more to be done that night, they cantered away to the church steeple. There they slept as before, though the sighs of the children disturbed them more than ever.

The next morning they betook themselves to the castle, almost as anxious about the Queen as about the shoe. They found her pale but composed, while the King gently argued with her about the jewel.

"But it really *is* perfect," said the King. "There is no other like it in the world. The missing diamond is only a sort of mark of its uniqueness. It is part of its perfection—if you could only see it that way."

"But I can't," said the Queen, with the greatest gentleness. "If it please your Majesty, we will present it to the Royal Museum. I only wanted Something Perfect. I have plenty of everything else."

How Stocking's heart sank when he heard that! Gleam's very own shoe would be locked up in the Royal Museum. It would always be between walls, never to be taken out where he might somehow have a

chance to get it! And he felt still more discouraged when he saw the King put it into a strong-box, and entrust it to two gentlemen of the castle. They were to take it under guard and deposit it in the Royal Museum.

Sadly he and Gleam followed along after the King's gentlemen. Sadly they saw the strong-box delivered to the Keeper of the Museum. And almost despairingly, that afternoon, looking through the strong bars that protected the windows, they saw it installed in a special case decorated with the king's crest and draped with the royal colors.

If Stocking had been the sort to give up, he would certainly have given up then, and gone back defeated to the castle of Saint Nicholas. But the thought of all the children in the world, discovering day by day that the calendar was stuck tight, and the sight of poor Gleam, pawing mournfully as he gazed through the window at his lost though honored shoe, revived his determination. There might be a way yet. They would watch for it.

That night they slept as usual on the church steeple. At least, Gleam slept. Stocking could only toss about and think. It was a cold winter night for the earth, so cold, indeed, that it seemed fresh even to him. One by one the lights went out in the houses and palaces. Fewer and fewer sounded the footsteps, farther apart the fits of barking from the palace watch dogs. Only the cats prowled over the snowy roofs, looking with their green eyes at the moon.

Suddenly Stocking noticed a stealthy light moving along the wall of the Royal Museum. Instantly he awakened Gleam. In a moment they were careening silently over the housetops. He did not know yet just what was happening, but whatever it was, it might bring the chance they were awaiting.

When they reached the museum, they saw—burglars! Two men with their hats down over their eyes and their cloaks drawn across their faces were digging the dirt away from an old, secret, underground door.

23

If only The Nature of Things would let Stocking creep in after them and snatch from them the reindeer's shoe! But no, he must wait until they came out and hope that they might drop it from haste or fear.

On the contrary, all seemed secure and quiet. The burglars even chuckled a little as they carried away the silver shoe with the rest of their booty. Gleam kicked his little heels frantically about on the cobblestones, hoping to frighten them. One of them did stop with a startled look, but the other said, after listening a moment, "It's only the frost." Tired and stiff, Gleam and Stocking followed the burglars to a dark hovel where they disappeared within a low, scowling door.

The dawn was already breaking then, and it seemed no use to try to go to sleep again on the church steeple. So Stocking and Gleam sprang up into the sky for a morning canter. There they met the hypogriffs who were just departing and followed the morning star to the edge of daybreak.

They came down from their gallop greatly heartened and refreshed. They had a better chance with burglars, Stocking reflected, than with shopkeepers and queens and Royal Museums and titled ladies with hundreds of servants. So they set themselves to watching the house where the burglars slept.

Presently the two men did come out again, and all day Stocking and Gleam trotted invisibly beside them. One was a handsome young gallant who should have been in better business. The other was as evil-looking as his way of life. Both wore black velvet capes, and fine broad hats with gay feathers.

All day they went about through the gayest streets of the city, spending freely and deporting themselves like fine gentlemen. But toward evening, when the early lamps were lighted, Stocking noticed that they were gradually making their way toward the meaner streets and alleys.

They stopped in a dark doorway, where they stood leaning against

25

the doorposts, glancing this way and that as if waiting for someone. And at last a third man joined them. They talked in a low tone, cautiously. In the dark of the doorway all three had their heads together, examining something sparkling by its own faint light.

Suddenly there was a shout, and a cry of "The King's Men! The King's Men!" Then a group of men wearing the king's uniform swooped down upon the burglars, and there was a great hue and cry. Burglars, King's Men, and onlookers darted in every direction. Two of the burglars were caught, but the youngest one made a dash for it. As he turned the corner at full speed something fell from his pocket onto the pavement

with a little ringing sound. There it lay, again in plain sight—Gleam's lost shoe!

Alas for poor Stocking! Just as he was about to swoop gleefully down upon it a little figure shot out of a nearby doorway, and Timmy's little brown fist snatched up the silvery jewel! Stocking was more disappointed than ever this time because he had come so near to recovering it.

It was growing late, now, and Timmy—who did not know how much his unseen friends wanted his treasure—would soon be going indoors to bed. And then a thought struck Stocking. Timmy did not look as if he lived within walls at all. And, as it turned out, Stocking was quite right. Sometimes Timmy slept with one of the scullery boys he knew. Sometimes he slept in the garret of Granny Goodwin, who kept the apple-stand. Usually, however, he slept wherever he happened to be.

Stocking's heart grew lighter and lighter as he followed Timmy. The boy was making his way down toward the wharf. There he knew of a big, empty box that had been left by the men unloading the ships. Turned on its side, it would make a fine shelter for the night.

Down the steep cobbled streets to the wharf Stocking and Gleam followed Timmy. When he reached the wharf he quickly found the box and stoutly jerked it into place. There was a little straw in the bottom, and this Timmy took as a further proof of his good luck. Having arranged it to his satisfaction, he curled himself up in the corner. He then lay looking at the strange, wonderful thing he had found.

Stocking chuckled to himself as he watched. For the first time since the accident, he began to feel like his natural self. Timmy would soon be asleep. Then there would be nothing in The Nature of Things to keep him from slipping the reindeer's shoe out of the lad's grimy little hand. For there were no walls about Timmy!

Very soon Timmy was asleep, smiling a little so that you could see the gap where the two teeth were missing. And then Stocking slipped the silvery shoe out of Timmy's hand. But before he sprang upon Gleam's back to race home to the castle of Saint Nicholas, he put a magic copper luckpiece in the hollow of Timmy's palm. It would take another story to tell you of all the good fortune which this luckpiece brought to Timmy.

As for Stocking and Gleam, they sprang into the air with a silvery shout and jingle. As they did, all the calendars in the world started off with a whirring sound to make up for lost time. It was Christmas Eve by the time they reached St. Nicholas's castle. Everything there had been ready for weeks, just waiting for Gleam to find his shoe.

Gleam was shod again in a hurry, and it was only a few minutes after midnight when the Saint set out on his rounds.

So, after all, things happened that year just as they always do on Christmas Eve. And all the children in the world—and Stocking—and Gleam—and Timmy—were happy at last.

28

THE REACHING PRINCESS

There was once a man named Tome, who lived in a waste place on the outskirts of a city. He cared for nothing but the books which filled his tumble-down hut. The books were full of wisdom, but since Tome was too lazy to share it with others, or even to enjoy it himself, he was neither happy nor wise. Indeed, he was as dour and dull as the trash heaps nearby.

A little way down the gully from his hut there lived an old witch-woman named Schnizzi, with her lumpish son, Glumpuddle. One morning Tome went to Schnizzi and said, "I need somebody to bring in the faggots for my fire and to carry water and to boil my lentils and cabbage. Get me someone."

"Humph," said Schnizzi. "If you will look in the tallest book on your upper-left-hand shelf you will find out how to get it all done by Black Magic."

"Humph, yourself," said Tome. "Are you going to tell me what's in my own books? As it happens, I don't want to do it by Black Magic. You

know very well that there are meddlers about. Palmers with their
cockle-shells, and peddlers with their packs, and those silly old priests
who are forever trotting by on their errands. They gape at my books,
and suppose that I am very pious. But the slaves who come out here to
dump the refuse from the city already suspect that you and I are versed
in Black Magic. If they see too much, they will tell tales. No, I must
have something human to bring in my faggots, and draw the water and
boil my cabbage and lentils. Get me one."

Then old Schnizzi sat down on her door stone with her sharp chin in
her sharp claws and thought and thought and thought. As she thought
she scratched queer signs in the dirt with a crooked stick she always
carried. All at once she gave a cackle and went sailing off into the air on
her stick.

The next morning when Tome woke up, a little girl was sitting on the
three-legged stool before the fire, poking up the faggots to make the
kettle boil. She was a beautiful little girl, with lips like scarlet maple-
keys and with curls as black as a tree trunk in the snow. But her eyes
were wide and frightened, with a kind of lost look in them.

"What is your name?" asked Tome.

"I don't know," said the little girl, in a soft, frightened voice.

"Don't know?" said Tome, testily. "Where did you come from, then?"

"I don't know," said the little girl again, looking still more frightened.

"Don't know, don't know, don't know," muttered Tome crossly, getting out of bed and sticking his skinny bare feet into his cold, shivery
slippers. No doubt he would have been crosser still, only he suspected
that Schnizzi knew more about all of this than the little girl ever would.
"Well, can you make porridge?"

"I—I can try," said the little girl, softly.

"Make some, then," said Tome; and putting on his shabby old robe
and cap he went out of the hut and down the gully to find Schnizzi.

Schnizzi was sitting on her door-stone, waving her crooked stick in

34

queer, slow figures at the rising sun. Her eyes blinked wickedly. Nearby, all in a lump, sat Glumpuddle.

"Where did you get her?" asked Tome.

"Don't you like her?" returned Schnizzi, grinning.

"That remains to be seen," answered Tome. "What's her name?"

Schnizzi's wicked old mind was so full of pleasure in her prank that she could not keep it to herself, and so, after she had teased him a while longer she told him all about it.

There was a king, she said, who ruled over a neighboring country, against whom she had an old grudge. His queen was dead and he had only one young daughter whom he was training up to succeed him as wise ruler over the kingdom. The little princess had hair as black as the trunk of a tree in the snow and lips like the keys of the scarlet maple. She was wise and good and merry, besides. The king took such pride in his daughter, that it was all a body could do, Schnizzi said, to endure having her alive.

For a long time Schnizzi had wanted to do the king a bad turn. Tome's need of a servant had suggested a way to do it, by carrying off the king's daughter. It was beyond Schnizzi's power to do the child any bodily harm, but she had managed to steal her memory, and had given it to Glumpuddle for a plaything.

As Schnizzi told her tale, Glumpuddle opened his hand and showed Tome a small, smooth, round stone, like a moonstone, with lovely lights and shadows in it.

Tome smiled sourly. So that was why the little girl did not know her name nor where she had come from.

"Well," he asked again, "What is her name?"

"Her name *was* Tensa," said Schnizzi, "when she was a princess. Now that she is only a drudge, we will call her Faggotty."

That was how Faggotty came to live among the ash-heaps and refuse-dumps on the outskirts of the city. She had no friends in the world but only dull, dour Tome and wicked old Schnizzi and the loutish Glumpuddle. And very sorry friends they were. To be sure, they never beat her, nor starved her, nor tried to make her learn or practice Black Magic. So long as she stayed about Tome's hut, and did the work that was expected of her, they let her go pretty much her own way.

36

THE REACHING PRINCESS

When Faggotty began to get used to her surroundings, she soon began to find things to enjoy and be happy over. She had lost her memory, you see, so she was spared grieving for her lost palaces and gardens and for her noble father, the king. And she didn't remember knowing any people who were handsomer or kinder than Tome and Schnizzi and Glumpuddle. To be sure, she sometimes saw better-looking people passing by, and sometimes a traveller with courteous manners stopped to ask for a drink of water. But wayfarers were few, and the look of Tome's hut was such that even fewer were moved to stop.

THE REACHING PRINCESS

Although Schnizzi had stolen Faggotty's memory, she had not stolen her kind and happy heart. The little Princess Tensa had already learned to be happy in a palace where there was much tedious ceremony and much decorous sitting still and many long lessons for one who must grow up to be a wise and good queen. And so, after a little while, it was easy for Faggotty to begin learning to be happy in a hut.

She learned to find treasures even in the trash heaps. She took in a brown rabbit who came limping over the ashes one day, lame, because the dogs had had him. She made him a hutch of withes woven together, and nursed him, and fed him with the outside cabbage leaves she set aside for him when she was cooking Tome's dinner. She gave him water daily in an old can lid. It was a happy day when she found a battered silver dish among the trash. She loved it the moment she set eyes upon it. Carefully she hammered out the dents, and polished it and gave it to Tremolo, the rabbit, to drink from.

Another day she found a bit of gold lace, which she pinned upon her ragged dress with a thorn. It made her feel like a queen. A little later she found an old broken lute with only one string. Hugging it joyfully, she danced down the gully to ask Glumpuddle to mend it for her.

Glumpuddle grinned and tossed her little memory-moonstone in his flat, leathery paws. Faggotty didn't know what his plaything was, and he would never let her look at it closely. "It's mine now," he would tease. "It's not yours any more. It's mine."

Plainly, she would get no help from Glumpuddle. She ran back to Tome's hut and did what she could to patch the lute herself. She cleaned it and tightened the one string until she could make sounds that pleased her and Tremolo, at least.

There was nothing else in Tome's hut

to please the ear or eye. Besides the books, the bed and Faggotty's pallet, there was a rickety table and chair, a three-legged stool and the pots and kettles with which Faggotty cooked the meals. She almost hated the pots and kettles. The only reason that she didn't *quite* hate them was because they were a sort of company for her.

As it was, she got terribly tired of them and would have given anything to be allowed to sit in a corner under the one dim, narrow, window, studying Tome's books. There were all sorts of books—tall ones and short ones, spilling out of the shelves and lying in dusty piles on the floor. Faggotty peeped into them whenever she had the chance. She could see that they were full of wisdom, and wisdom, she thought, ought to make a person happy and useful. She yearned to understand them better.

But whenever Tome caught her looking into his books, he would lift her up by a curl and tell her gruffly to go and bring in the wood or the water, or to cook him some lentils or porridge. Once or twice she summoned up courage to ask him to explain something she had read in the books. But Tome brushed her away, grumbling, "What does a girl want with learning? In a few years you'll be old enough to marry Glumpuddle, and you know more than he does, already."

When he made such a terrible threat as that, Faggotty was glad enough to run back to her pots and kettles. The old, round, black pot looked a little like Glumpuddle, for that matter, but at least she need never think of marrying it. As she lifted and scrubbed and scraped every day, Faggotty sang to herself,

> "Pot and kettle
> Try your mettle."

and pretended that there was a contest between her and the pots, who were trying to make her mind as dull and dumpy and black as they were. Usually, she won the contest, for she had made up her mind not to wash Tome's pots and kettles forever.

39

She didn't see how in the world she was ever to get away from them, though, or where she was to go. But something told her that there must be other and better places than where she was and better things to do than marrying Glumpuddle. If she tried hard enough she could find them. This hope kept her searching the pages of Tome's books.

Tome often napped during the day after studying late into the night. As time went on, Faggotty found more time to read while the old man drowsed. Some of Tome's books were queer, indeed. These were books about Magic—White, Grey and Black Magic, and all shades in between. But since the color of the magic depends principally upon the color of the reader's eyes, Faggotty learned hardly anything but White Magic.

Whenever, now and then, she happened to get a little speck of Black Magic stuck on her mind, she would take it to the back door and shake it until it was clean again—just as she shook out daily Tome's ragged hearth-rug.

And thus days and years passed, but Faggotty managed to keep alive her courage and her longing. Each year she was able to reach higher on Tome's bookshelves. She began to suspect that the wisest books were on the tallest shelves, so she kept reaching.

Most evenings, after Faggotty had given Tome his supper, and put the pots and kettles away, she would go out and sit on the door stone and watch the pictures the sun made in his setting. And over and over again she would see castles and palaces in the piled-up clouds. Although she had lost her memory, there was something about those cloud-castles that called to her and hurt her heart. As time went on, they seemed to tell her more and more about things that she had once known, known long ago and forgotten.

One evening as she was watching the sunset clouds, they seemed so near that she reached out to touch them. Just then, Schnizzi came riding by on her crooked stick. Faggotty almost never asked anything of Schnizzi, for she knew what a cruel old thing she was. This time,

41

however, she could not help saying, "I know *I* must have lived in a palace, Schnizzi! Oh, Schnizzi, how can I get back to my palace?"

The witch-woman darted at her the queerest look you can imagine, a look that was part triumph and part fear. "Highty-tighty!" she cried. "Talking of palaces! You'll live in Glumpuddle's palace, my dear. That's where you'll live—for all your reaching!"

After that there was no peace for Faggotty. Every day something was said about her marrying Glumpuddle. She was a tall girl now, and the face that she saw in the well when she went to draw water told her that she was nearly as grownup as the young country wives who passed once in a while, taking a short cut into the city with their baskets on their heads.

And Glumpuddle was always at her heels. He never had much to say for himself. He would only follow her around, and whenever she stopped to rest he would sit down in a lump on a stone nearby and open his hand that had her memory in it and sit grinning at it. Poor Faggotty was sick with terror. And yet she *knew* that she would never marry Glumpuddle. She would find some way of escape, but when and how she did not know.

More and more she pored over Tome's books. And now, just when she needed them most, she discovered that at last she could reach the wisest books on the topmost shelf.

One evening, when Tome was asleep in his chair, and Schnizzi had taken Glumpuddle off on some bad errand, Faggotty came upon a wisdom in an old book that made her heart flutter in her throat. This wisdom was wrapped up in curious symbols, and it was in a learned language she had only half mastered, but it seemed to mean that if a maiden in need could make herself known to a white heron with one blue feather, flying at night between the clouds and the moon, there might be help for her.

Then Faggotty knew that she must go seek that help if she were ever to be free of the hut and the trash heaps and lazy old Tome and wicked old Schnizzi and that lump of a Glumpuddle.

Late that night Faggotty stole out of Tome's hut. She had left the pots and kettles in order and the water jugs filled and the faggots laid in the fireplace for the morning fire. She took nothing with her but the ragged clothes she was wearing, a crust of the bread she had baked the day before, and her rabbit, Tremolo, whom she carried under her cloak.

As she left, she stopped in the path and looked back at the hut. The moon was shining, picking out, even now, something here and there among the waste to glitter upon. And then she took a deep breath and sped like a shadow—not knowing where she was going, or how, but only that she must make herself known to a white heron with one blue feather, flying at night between the clouds and the moon.

At last she came to the highway leading into the city. She passed in, wondering, for she had never seen a city before, or at least she thought she had not. By then, dawn had come, fresh and rosy. Everything looked its best. She would have liked to stay in the city, with its shops and palaces and gardens, but she didn't see anything there that seemed likely to help her find the white heron with one blue feather. So, after stopping to rest and share her crust of bread with Tremolo, she pressed on.

She found her way out of the city and into the country again. The

birds were caroling and the air was fresh. Having put such a distance between herself and Glumpuddle, she felt quite gay and hopeful. As she walked, she sang,

"Seek what you need,
Listen and heed,
Hope is speed."

Then, out of nowhere, came a swishing whistle behind her like an angry wind. It was Schnizzi on her crooked stick, swooping down on her!

The witch woman leaped from her stick and brandished it at Faggotty. "The reaching girl!" she screamed. "Too good for my Glumpuddle! Reaching for palaces, palaces, palaces!" She made a hateful, scornful song of it, ending in a screech, "I'll settle you! I'll give you enough of reaching!"

She struck Faggotty with the crooked stick, and there, right in the middle of the highway, the maiden was turned into a tree!

She was a tall, beautiful tree, with a straight trunk and long, up-stretching branches trembling in the morning breeze. Schnizzi careened around and around in the air above her, beside herself with triumph. "Reach, reach, reach!" she screeched. "Reach the birds down out of the sky!" With a long malicious cackle, she whirled and whizzed back the way she had come.

Faggotty was left standing in the highway, no longer Faggotty, but a beautiful tree. Her heart, within the straight, dark trunk, was the same as ever. Schnizzi could never change that, for all her spite. But Faggotty's mind, of course, was bewildered beyond measure. For a while she could only sway and shiver in amazement, feeling lost and alone.

Pretty soon she felt a soft, eager throbbing at her feet, and there was Tremolo, nestling in the grass that was already beginning to grow about her roots. From that moment she began to feel comforted. Her

46

heart crept out of the dark trunk and up into the high branches. How far she could see from there! How friendly the sky was, and how blue! A bird came and perched on one of her boughs, cocking his bright eye and looking about, pleased and surprised at finding a tree where only the highway had been before.

Two ox-carts, one behind the other, and both loaded with wood, came creaking down the road toward the city. When they came close to where the tree was, the first carter drew up his team with a loud "Whoa!" The one behind him stopped, too.

"What do you make of this, friend?" asked the first carter. "A tree in the middle of the highway! Why, there was no tree here a week ago."

"You're right about that, neighbor," said the second carter. "What a strange thing! And a fine large tree it is. It would make a great heap of firewood. Do you think, now, we ought to cut it down, and clear the highway of it?"

The first carter puzzled about it a little. "No, I don't think so, " he decided. "I'm thinking it's some notion the king has taken, to have this fine tree brought from his forests, and set out at night in the highway as if it had always grown here, for everybody's wonder and admiration. No, I'm thinking we'd get into a fine pickle if we cut down the king's tree."

So the first carter drove to the right, and the second to the left, leaving the tree in a sort of island in the highway. And all the travellers who came after drove either to the left or to the right, looking up at the branches of the tree and marvelling at this new fancy of the king's. At last there were two plain roads, one on each side of the tree, so that nobody thought that it should be otherwise.

All this time the heart and mind of Faggotty were learning to live quite happily within the tree. To be sure, she grew more and more anxious to be going on. Sometimes she would tremble all over with impatience to continue her search. "I *must* find a white heron with one

48

blue feather, flying between the clouds and the moon," she told Tremolo. "I *must* go on."

Tremolo sat back on his haunches to look up into her branches. "Well, now, " he deliberated. "I wonder. Seems to me you might be more likely to find what you seek by going up than by going on."

This seemed like sensible advice; and, in any case, there was little else to be done at the moment. So the tree began to reach, putting her mind to growing taller and taller. I don't mean that she didn't take time to enjoy the tree-happiness of blossom time and leaf time and seed time, or to talk to Tremolo among the tall grass at her feet, or to rock the baby birds in their nests among her branches. She enjoyed all of these things, and she was almost happy. But as the tree grew, so did her determination not to be a tree always, and her feeling that the thing for her to do was to keep on reaching, higher and higher, until she could see between the clouds and the moon.

Folk going along the highway just after sunset on winter evenings would see the tree standing there against the light in the west, reaching and reaching. And some would feel flat and unaspiring in comparison, and decide to reach a little harder, themselves. And that was good for them. Others thought, "How still that tree is while it reaches—and how calm." And that made them more patient, which was good for the people they lived with. As for the reaching tree, she sang over and over to herself a happy little tune she had learned from a passing skylark:

"The way to be high
Is to try and try."

For three whole years the reaching tree stood in the middle of the highway and reached. When the fourth winter set in, she began to feel discouraged, in spite of the fact that she had really grown a lot. Finally, on a night of frosty moonlight, she felt so downhearted that she just gave up and drooped a little, as you do sometimes.

"I've done my best," she sighed. "I've tried awfully hard. But I just

49

can't see up above the clouds. I need wings—or sharper eyes—or anyway, something, that I haven't got."

While Tremolo was wondering how he could help her get back her courage, a Great Horned Owl came sailing softly toward the tree on his broad, noiseless wings. He flew in among her branches, and settled himself in a dark place against her trunk. Down among her roots, Tremolo carefully kept out of sight and waited to see what would happen next.

The owl was such a solemn person that the reaching tree waited for him to speak first. But for quite some time he just sat there, without a wink of his great round eyes, staring straight up at the white clouds that turned to gold as they slipped across the face of the moon. Presently, he hooted in his muffled voice,

> "Who, who, who are you?
> Who are you,
> Feather-of-Blue?"

Hearing this, Tremolo understood that magic was abroad that night and that it was White Magic, so he didn't need to be afraid. The night was so still you could hear the twigs snap in the frost, and through the stillness came a far-off, answering cry.

Once more the owl hooted up at the shining clouds:

> "True, true, waits for you,
> Reaches for you,
> Feather-of-Blue!"

And then, down through the shining night, the tree, the owl and the rabbit saw a white heron sailing. White as silver he was in the moonlight, with one feather of iridescent blue on his shoulder. Down, down, down he came, while the watchers below waited breathlessly. And just as the reaching tree felt she could bear it no longer for hope and wonder, the heron folded his wide wings and settled down among her topmost branches.

51

And now the magical wisdom she had puzzled out of Tome's old book came true. She made herself known to the White Heron with one blue feather, and asked his help in her great need. In joyful wonder she listened as the heron told her about her father, the king, and how he had been grieving for his lost daughter these many years. And he told her how the king had looked and looked for her the wide world over, and how, when all else had failed, he had sent for the White Heron and the Great Horned Owl to continue the search.

Tremolo, pressed warmly against the foot of the tree, listened with quivering nose and ears. Feeling him there, the tree-princess was reminded of the deep roots that held her to the earth.

"But I am still a tree," she cried out. "And I have no memory of my father or my kingdom or my name. What am I to do?"

So the heron thought and the owl thought and Tremolo thought and the tree-princess thought deeply, while the frosty wind sighed through her branches. Presently, little Tremolo spoke up, "That wicked old

Schnizzi must have stolen your memory when she stole you away from your kingdom."

At that, the tree-princess remembered the little milky moonstone that Glumpuddle used to play with, and how he used to tease her, saying that it had once belonged to her but was now his very own. She wondered, "Could that be my memory?"

Her friends agreed that it was very likely. They agreed, too, that her memory must be found and restored to her, if she were ever to become Princess Tensa again.

The White Heron made ready to take to the air once more. The owl and Tremolo wanted to go with him, but he bade them stay and care for the princess while he was gone.

He watched for a break in the silvery clouds, then lifted his wings, rose from the branch where he had rested, and sailed aloft, turning from white to silver in the moonlight. They gazed after him until he vanished between the clouds and the moon.

Three days and three nights passed by slowly. The tree-princess was most grateful for the company of the Great Horned Owl and Tremolo, and they did all they possibly could to cheer her, but it took all she had learned as a princess and as a drudge and as a tree to be patient and calm and brave now while she waited.

Just before daybreak of the fourth morning, the White Heron returned. He glided down to meet the upstretched branches of the reaching tree, and she saw that he carried the memory-moonstone in his beak. As it touched the tallest twig of her tallest branch she felt a marvelous change. And lo! as an icicle crashes into a thousand diamonds, the tree—roots, trunk, branches, twigs and all—fell into fragments, and there stood Princess Tensa, with lips like scarlet maple keys and hair as black as a tree trunk in the snow, dressed in royal robes. The heron laid the moonstone in her hand, and she remembered her life as Princess Tensa.

The very next moment, with a jingle of harness and drumming of hoofbeats, her father, the good old king, with his men-at-arms in his train, came along the highway to meet her. And who should be guiding them but Glumpuddle!

Together at long last, the Princess Tensa and her grateful king-father set out for their own kingdom. With them went Tremolo in the Princess's arms, while the Great White Heron and the Great Horned Owl flew on either side of the cavalcade.

To pass the time on the journey, the heron was asked to tell the company how he had rescued Princess Tensa's memory. This is how it happened:

The White Heron had found Glumpuddle alone, and had easily persuaded him to give up the moonstone in exchange for the beautiful blue feather he wore on his shoulder. Glumpuddle had been so proud of his new treasure, in fact, that he had fastened it on his jacket over his heart, begging to be allowed to go to the good king's kingdom and enter the royal service.

Before the two could leave the gully, however—the heron continued his tale—the witch woman, Schnizzi, had swooped down upon them. "Rob me, will you?" she screeched. "We'll see about that!" And hopping off her crooked stick, she had flailed it at the White Heron like a windmill gone mad.

With mighty wings and stout beak, the heron had met the attack. He broke the magic stick with a c-r-r-r-ack! leaving Schnizzi powerless. Then, sending Glumpuddle ahead to guide the king to their meeting place, he had hastened back to the princess with her long-lost memory.

The heron's story helped pass the time pleasantly on the journey to Princess Tensa's kingdom. Her happy people welcomed the princess royally, and received her friends with high honors. The owl was made Exalted Leading Owl and Tremolo was named Esteemed Royal Rabbit. The White Heron was appointed Chief High Councillor of the Realm.

54

Glumpuddle became a doorman at the palace, and proudly wore the blue heron-feather on his uniform. His heart was not as stupid as his mind; so he was able to learn good new ways as he forgot the bad old ones.

The good old king lived and ruled to a hearty old age. And when he died, he was glad to leave his kingdom to his daughter, who ruled over it with her three wise councillors for long, illustrious years.

Queen Tensa never forgot the time when she had lived as a drudge among the trash heaps, and the slow seasons she had spent reaching so ardently in the tree. And she was glad that she had taken Tremolo's advice and kept on reaching. For truly, she had found what she sought by going up rather than by going on.

THE STORM KING'S PLUME

Carl, the younger son of the king's forester, was lame. His older brother, Matthew, was strong and rosy. Matthew could go racketing over the mountain roads on his stout white pony, helping his father guard the king's deer. But little pale Carl sat all day long looking across the valley to the mountain-ridge on the opposite side.

Carl's seat was a great chair like a throne. Matthew had made it for him, working on rainy days and winter evenings. His mother had padded it with cushions and set it out under the pear tree.

Their little stone house nestled in a hollow where the side of the mountain was like a great, grassy shoulder. Carl could see for millions of leagues, he thought, on a clear day. Over his head the old pear tree changed as the months went around. In late March it looked as if it were covered with popcorn. Early in April the round, white, swelling buds burst into a foam which had a perfume as sweet as honey and which hummed all day long with bees. Here, all through the pleasant weather, Carl watched and listened and hummed along with them.

Soon the white foam above Carl's head was gone, and tight little pears were set in bunches of bright green leaves. Then, through the warm, drowsy days of midsummer he could fancy that he saw them swelling and rounding, and he knew that he could see the gold spreading over their burnished cheeks. And at last, with the autumn, they began to grow ripe and fall, and his mother gathered most of them and made them into honey-colored preserves. But she always left a few in the grass around his chair. She knew that he loved to watch the many creatures who came to sip the sun-brewed cider that oozed out of their sides.

There were bumble-bees with yellow breeches, and blue-winged flies, and green-backed beetles. Best of all he liked the brown butterflies, who looked as if his mother had snipped the velvet of their angled wings all around the edges with her scissors. Carl had grown very well acquainted with all these visitors. His mother used to smile to herself sometimes as she went about her work, to hear him talking with them. They told him stories and taught him songs that other people could not hear.

All sorts of interesting persons came to pay Carl sudden visits as he sat under the pear tree. Little striped gophers and tremulous white-tailed rabbits and squirrels who were very knowing and full of news. And birds—oh, any number of birds!

Lizards came too. And sometimes even, in the hot noons, when he was almost dozing in the heavy, sweet air, a snake would come sliding around a rock. It would stop nearby in a motionless coil, with its slim head lifted and its brilliant glittering eyes fastened upon him. Carl was not afraid of the snakes. He loved to watch them. He lay back in his big chair, almost as motionless as they, answering their queer, cold talk and learning their silent songs, without so much as opening his lips.

But there was one thing he was afraid of. He was afraid of the storms

60

that sometimes came rushing and crashing over the mountains. They bellowed up the gorges and shut away from him with curtains of wild rain the wide, colorful view that he loved. Sometimes a flash of lightning would show him some distant corner of his valley, with its little trees lashed wildly about. He almost wept to think of the tiny flowers being trampled under the cruel flying feet of the Storm King.

Yet when such storms came, he was drawn, in spite of himself, to the window, to watch the tumult outside. He cowered there with terrified eyes, but every time the thunder crashed or the lightning darted through the darkness he would shiver and hide his face in his hands for fear he might actually see the terrible Storm King.

Now Carl's father, Michael, the king's forester, was a great-shouldered, windy-voiced man who had never been tired in his life or afraid of anything. He could not understand why he should have had a little pale-faced boy who was lame. His son Matthew was his companion and right hand. Michael delighted in seeing him prove his strength and hardihood before the other foresters who lived on the other side of the mountain. But he never looked at Carl if he could help it.

On bright days, when Michael would come singing up the path, leading his surefooted black horse by its jingling bridle-rein, he would sometimes toss Carl a sweetmeat or a penny, and, with it, a word or two. But he never stopped by Carl's chair, and his eyes always passed on as quickly as possible. The worst of it was that Carl would rather have had his father lay his hand on his head than be noticed by the king himself. He thought there was no man in the world as great as his father.

In the daytime, as Michael came and went about his work, it was natural enough that he did not notice Carl, for he was busy then. But there were long winter evenings when Michael and Matthew would talk over their next day's plans or their day's adventures. Carl would sit by his mother's spinning wheel, trying to listen to the stories she told

62

him, but quite unable to keep his thoughts from wandering to the talk of Matthew and his father.

He would never be able, he thought, to do anything to make his father proud of *him*, as he was of Matthew. And on stormy nights it was the worst of all. For then his father would turn and see Carl crouching by the window, and he would say, in a stern voice, "Take the boy away from the window, Peg!"

Then Carl's mother would lift her eyes pleadingly to his face and say in a low voice, "But he does not want to move, husband! Let him be!"

At that Carl's father would turn his back and busy himself again over his mending of crossbow or saddle-girth. But when the next thunder crash came, he would spring up, and seizing his green forester's cape and cap, he would rush out into the downpour, slamming the door behind him.

Presently Carl would catch the sound of his voice above the storm, roaring out a forester's song far down the mountainside. Then he would give a little sob, half of sorrow, half of relief, for he knew that his father had been able to forget having a little crippled son at home who was afraid.

But the storms did not come very often, and on the long, sunny days Carl was happy. Then, you see, he was able to forget that his father did not like to look at him. There were always so many other things to think about then, and so much to be seen from his chair under the old pear tree. Besides the things I have told you about, the clouds and the shadows of them were enough to keep him happy all day long. There were cliffs he knew by name, which the shifting lights often seemed to turn into friendly stone faces which smiled benignly upon him across the blue haze of the valley. And there were clumps of woods here and there, each of its own shape and color, which looked different at different hours of the day, but which never looked like each other.

There were even single trees that he knew as friends. There was the sturdy little thorn tree in the crevice of the rock. There was a proud twisted snag that had once been a great oak. There was a cedar which had a ragged grace like that of a sailing ship with torn rigging.

And there was a pine.

The pine was, indeed, the best-loved of all Carl's friends. It stood quite alone on the bare ridge of the mountain directly across the valley from his home, and it made him think of a splendid green plume.

64

Matthew, whom he had asked about it once, had told him that it was an enormous tree, far too large for Matthew himself to reach around, even with his long arms. But from where Carl sat it looked so slender and graceful that it made him laugh sometimes to think how easily a giant might snap it off and stick it in his cap. Its trunk was not a perfectly straight column, like that of most pines, but sprang aside a little, in a sort of playful curve, a little way above the ground. That was the place for the giant to snap it. But Carl wouldn't have laughed if he had thought a giant would ever do it, for he felt that the tree was his very own.

In the sky beyond the pine he saw his most gorgeous cloud-pictures. The sun set there, and so, evening after evening Carl watched wonders without end pass as in a procession behind his sun-gilded, steadfast tree. Sometimes there were islands of pure gold in a sea of azure, sometimes billowing cloud-mountains with castles on their heads.

Sometimes there were glorious monsters out of an untold fairy tale—pawing horses, and whales and dragons, and crouching lions with the humps of camels. And then, as these swift things faded and the flaming pictures melted into the quiet sea of the last calm light, there still stood, silent and friendly, as long as there was light to see, his comrade who lived across the valley—the pine tree that he called the Plume.

One May morning, as Carl was sitting in his accustomed place, he saw a big black crow come winging across the valley, straight from the pine tree, calling, "Car-r-rl, Car-r-rl, Car-r-rl!" as he came. Carl had often watched birds flying back and forth, as if they had a blue, invisible highway from one mountain top to the other, but this was the first time he had ever heard one call him by name.

The crow came on as Carl watched, and after circling around above his head, still calling to attract his attention, he came directly down and seated himself beside him on a low branch of the pear tree. Nobody was about except Carl. His mother was singing softly as she worked in her

66

herb-bed on the other side of the house, and his father and Matthew were off among the steep mountain ways looking after the king's beasts.

Clearing his throat hoarsely, the crow looked all about him, as if he had something to say, but did not know where to begin. "I've come to discuss a matter with you," he said at last.

"What is it?" asked Carl.

"The Storm King," said the Crow, "wants your Plume to wear in his hat."

For several moments Carl did not say a word. He was so completely surprised, you see. He was so afraid of the Storm King and his cruel and terrible ways. Why should he be asked to give up to him the thing which, next to his father and mother and Matthew, he loved best in all the world?

"He's going a-wooing," said the Crow, as Carl did not speak. "He's going a-wooing the Lady Who Lives in the Lightnings. She's very bright, they tell me—quite dazzling. And the Storm King is mad about her. And he wants your Plume to wear in his purple hat."

"I don't want him to have my Plume," said Carl at last, in a very low voice that was close to tears. "I want to keep my Plume. And I don't like the Storm King."

"Well!" said the Crow. He stuck his hands into the hip-pockets under his black coattails and sat looking up at the sky through the branches of the pear tree, as if for inspiration.

"I told him you wouldn't want to give it up," he said at last. "And I told him I was no hand at making speeches. No orator—no orator at all."

"What did he say then?" asked Carl, looking up in spite of himself out of the corner of his eye.

"Oh, he just told me to fly along anyhow, and look about and see what I could do."

"Well," said Carl suddenly, straightening up in spite of his crooked

67

knee, and speaking more determinedly than he had ever done before in his life, "you may just go back and tell the Storm King I won't do it."

"By George!" said the Crow. And he took his hands from under his coattails and went flapping straight back across the valley.

Carl watched him go. After a little while he just couldn't help smiling.

The Storm King had chosen a pretty poor messenger, he thought! He might have sent a bird who could sing, if he couldn't find one to deliver a real speech. The Storm King would never persuade him to do anything at this rate—certainly never to give him his Plume that he wanted so much to keep.

Then he began to remember what a terrible person the Storm King must be. Although he had never seen him, he had heard his awful voice, and he had seen the trees on the mountain side crash under his footsteps. Why, the Storm King could curl his little finger about the Plume and snap it clean off. Or he could come and blow Carl himself down into the gorge without so much as puffing out his cheeks.

Then Carl felt something he had never felt before. He felt his little heart, which had never in his life stood up against anybody, stand up within him and say, "No, I will not give up to the Storm King! He has the power to take my beautiful Plume if he wishes, but he can't frighten me into giving it to him!" Nevertheless, that night Carl tossed and moaned a little in his sleep, and his mother got up to straighten the pillow under his head and see if he was covered from the chill of the night.

But the next morning he was settled bright and early in his chair under the pear tree. The morning mist was rolling up the valley, and a wisp of smoke was rising from the ledge far below him, where Matthew and his father had built a little fire. And again he saw the Crow flapping toward him, calling, "Car-r-rl, Car-r-rl, Car-r-rl!"

The Crow came down as before and seated himself on the limb of the pear tree. "The Storm King wants your Plume," he said.

Carl straightened up and spoke in an indignant, confident voice. "The Storm King is cruel," he said. "Why should I give up my Plume to deck the purple hat of a cruel king because he is going a-wooing?" You see he had been thinking up arguments in the night, all through his dreams.

"He isn't cruel," said the Crow, "not especially. He rackets and roars,

but noise doesn't hurt anybody. And, once in a while, he steps on a tree or a house, by mistake. Or drops one of the arrows out of his quiver and it goes through a man and kills him. But it's a sort of accident. The Storm King has nothing against 'em."

Carl sat silent. He wasn't convinced, but he didn't know what to say.

"Just like my eating up the little robins," said the Crow. "I've nothing against 'em. But I'm hungry."

"Yes, and it's wicked of you!" cried Carl, again plucking up spirit. Indeed, he had had this grievance against the Crow in the back of his mind all along, and he had always thought he would never speak to a bird that would do such a thing. But the Crow had looked so comical and so interesting, as he sat in the pear tree with his hands in his pockets, that he had let it pass.

Now the Crow said, "You eat partridges."

Carl hung his head. Indeed he did, but he made up his mind then and there that he would never do so again.

"We all have to do the best we can in this world," went on the Crow. "We all have our faults. I kill robins; men kill crows. The Storm King rackets around because it's his nature to; he told me to tell you so. He's only going about his business."

"Where do you live?" asked Carl, after a moment, since he could think of nothing else to say to change the subject.

"In the top of the pine tree you call your Plume," said the Crow. "The Storm King promised me, if I'd get you to give it to him, he'd wait till my children are grown before he takes it. Otherwise, he's likely to snap it off anytime, and they'll be spilled all over the mountain. The Storm King wants it to put in his purple hat. He's going a-wooing. He's mad about the Lady Who Lives in the Lightnings. She's very bright, they say—quite dazzling. She's —"

"You've said all that before," said Carl, crossly, for he was feeling very much perplexed.

70

"By George!" said the Crow. And he took his hands out of his pockets and went flapping back across the valley.

But the next morning at the usual time he came winnowing back with long, leisurely flaps, calling as before, "Car-r-rl, Car-r-rl, Car-r-rl!" And when he had alighted on the pear tree, he began as before, "The Storm King wants your Plume."

"Oh dear," said Carl. "I don't know what to do! I don't want your children to be spilled all over the mountain."

"I thought that would fetch you around," said the Crow. "It did me."

"But I want to keep my Plume," said Carl.

"The Storm King told me to tell you," said the Crow, "that if you let him have it, you shall *see* him wear it—and that will be a fine sight. He says, the next time you hear him about, you're to go to the window and look. Then you'll see him stepping across the mountains, with his black velvet cape billowing behind him, and the Plume waving over the crown of his purple hat with the rolling brim. Only, you're not to be afraid. If you're afraid you can't see him. And he says it will be a fine sight."

Here the Crow pushed his hat back on his forehead and took a long breath, as if he were glad to have finished reciting the speech the Storm King taught him.

For a long time Carl said nothing. Then he asked a little tremulously, "Does my Plume want to go?"

"By George!" said the Crow, quite taken by surprise. It was plain he had no instructions to cover that question. He pulled his hat down hard over his ears and went flapping back across the valley.

That evening, just about sunset, Carl still sat under the pear tree, looking across at his dear pine tree on the opposite ridge. He was feeling quite peaceful but quite sad, for he felt that he had almost made up his mind. He didn't understand all about it by any means, but somehow he had nearly decided that he ought to give his Plume to the Storm King.

A strong but quiet breeze had sprung up, not cold, but cool with the

72

searching spring coolness, as it swept up from the valley and curled briskly around the shoulder of the mountain. Carl knew that his mother would soon be taking him indoors. But before he went, he longed to know whether his Plume wanted to go.

At last he folded his hands in his lap and sent a message to the tree, where it stood so steadfast against the evening sky: "Oh beautiful Plume, do you wish me to let you go, that you may wave forever in the purple hat of the Storm King?"

And across the valley, as he watched, he saw the Plume gently bow its head as if it were saying "Yes."

The next morning he watched for the Crow, but he did not come. Neither did he come on the mornings afterward. Carl presently decided that he was busy teaching his children to fly. He was glad of this, for they would then be safe from the danger of being spilled all over the mountain. But it also gave him a little tremor around his heart, for it meant that the time was approaching for the Storm King to take the Plume for his purple hat. He wondered how the Storm King knew that he had given his consent, but he was sure that he did know, because he had left the Crow's nest undisturbed in the high branches of his tree.

A few weeks later, he was very much excited to see the Crow flapping once more across the valley, calling as before, "Car-r-rl, Car-r-rl, Car-r-rl!"

"Everything's settled," said the Crow, as he seated himself on the low limb of the pear tree. "I shut up the house today."

"Then the Storm King's going to take my Plume?" quavered Carl.

"As soon as the Lady Who Lives in the Lightnings comes back from her visit to the Comet. He's her cousin, you know. If you watch, some evening you'll see the Storm King's black velvet cape billowing up from the other side of the world —"

"Oh," cried Carl, and he could not keep the tears from coming into his eyes, "I'm glad he's going to have it, since it wants to go, and since he

74

didn't spill your children all over the mountain! And I want to see the grand sight he'll be, leaping over the gorges to go a-wooing, with my Plume waving in his purple hat. But I can't help grieving that I'll not see it any more across the valley—"

"By George!" interrupted the Crow, shuffling around on the branch most uncomfortably. "Do you have to do that?" he asked, all the while fumbling desperately in all his pockets as if he were looking for a pocket-handkerchief. Not finding any, he gave it up, and stepping abruptly off the limb, he went flapping back across the valley.

After that Carl watched for signs of the Storm King, and finally one evening he saw the folds of his cloak billowing up from behind the mountain. Just then the clothes began to blow off the clothesline and the shutters began to clatter and bang, and his mother came running up to carry him into the house. His father and Matthew came stamping in a moment later, and his mother lighted the lamp and began to bustle about getting supper.

Carl crept to the window to watch for the Storm King. Not crouching and cringing as he had always done before, but standing up on his chair as best he could, with quick-drawn breath and shining eyes.

Ah, if you could have seen what Carl saw that night! Splendid and strong like Carl's own father, the Storm King strode across the valley with his cape surging behind, and the Plume, the wonderful green Plume, waving over his purple hat. Carl saw him spring into the clouds to meet the dazzling Lady Who Lives in the Lightnings. There she stood above the mountain top, waiting for the Storm King, and Carl saw her throw aside the veil that hid her bright eyes as the Storm King seized her in his arms and went laughing down the valley with a voice like a cataract.

Carl, clapping his hands and laughing, had forgotten everybody inside of the little house till he heard his father's voice, saying, "'Sh! Look at the lad! What's come over him?" Then he turned and saw his

father standing stock-still, with his hand on his mother's arm. She, too, stood peering at Carl from under the lamp she held. Suddenly both of them came running toward him and shook him gently, laughing.

His mother said, "I told you he'd outgrow it, husband!"

But his father seized him bodily in his arms and swung him up on his shoulder as he had never done before, and marched around and around the room with him, crying again and again, "Look at him, Matthew! Look at him, Peg! No one's afraid in *this* house!"

His mother wiped her eyes on her apron and smiled, "No indeed, husband!" but added anxiously, "Take care you don't hurt him!" Then they all fell to laughing together.

Carl's life was quite different after that. He still spent much of his time in his chair under the pear tree, and sang with the birds, and the green beetles and the timid brown rabbits with white tails. The Crow never came back. The ridge where the Plume had been was quite bare, but Matthew, who often rode farther than that on a day's journey, told Carl that little pine seedlings were springing up all around the place where it had stood. The tree had been snapped off, he said, just at the point where the mighty trunk made a little playful swerve; and though he had looked and looked, he could see no trace of the great head of it in the gorge below. Carl knew why this should be, but he never explained it.

But the different part of his life was that his father talked and played with him whenever he had a chance. He made all sorts of games for him and little contrivances to help and encourage him to strengthen his crippled leg. And he began to take Carl behind him on his black horse for short journeys about the mountain.

And one day, while Carl was riding behind his father, they came upon the king, who was out with his train for a royal hunt. And the king's chief minstrel, who was riding at his bridle-rein, spied the little pale lame boy and got off his horse and came to talk with him. He was a wise

76

man who could read people's faces, and was not at all surprised when he found that Carl often talked to trees and snakes and beetles and birds and knew some of their songs. Presently he led Carl to the king himself, who, after he had spoken with him a little, asked him if he would like to come to his court to live and be trained as a minstrel.

And so it came about that, when Carl was old enough, he went to be a pupil of the king's minstrel. He grew up to be himself a very famous one, and was made the king's chief singer when the time came. When the king heard Carl sing the songs of the forest creatures, he no longer wished to hunt them, but gave them the freedom of his mountain kingdom, to be protected by the king's foresters forever.

Michael, who lived to be a hale old man, often boasted in the evenings as he smoked his long pipe with his cronies, about his son Matthew, who was a master-forester. But oftener still, he boasted of his younger son, Carl, who was a great minstrel, and lived at the king's court, but who never forgot his mother and his old father.

Carl's songs were sung in many countries. The most famous song of all told of how the Storm King had gone a-wooing the Lady Who Lives in the Lightnings and had won her heart by the magic of a certain green plume that crowned his purple hat. And this song was known at the courts of many kingdoms as "The Song of the Storm King's Plume."

'PILIO

There was once a little old lady who lived alone high up on the side of a mountain. The only relatives she had in the world were a tea-kettle, a tabby cat, and a cricket. To be sure, there was an old nanny goat, but she was more of a friend than a relative. And there was a hen named Hannah, but she was not much company, for she knew nothing about anything whatever except worms and eggs.

The little old lady's place on the side of the mountain was so very rocky that the place for the garden was hardly bigger than a pocket-handkerchief. Of course, it may have been a giant's pocket-handker-chief; the cricket didn't say what kind it was, the day I passed by that way and stopped to rest on the doorstep. The garden was behind the house and the old lady was in the garden, so all I have was the cricket's word for it. But, anyhow, it was a very small garden, just as it was a small house, and a very small old lady, and a very small tabby cat. The only thing about the whole premises that wasn't small was Hannah's cackle.

Now, the old lady had just the kind of faded, crinkled, rose-petally skin that all right-minded old ladies ought to have, and just the sort of old-blue eyes with puckered corners, and she wore just the sort of slippers—little soft, broad-toed slippers that made a quick, whispering flip-flop as she scuttled about the little old house. And of course she had white hair, and a ruffled cap, and was as neat as a waxwing.

As I have said, the little old lady had neither chick nor child in the world, but she had a bit of money in the old blue teapot in the chimney cupboard. It was enough to last out her time—living, as she did, in such a careful way. She had her garden, you see, and Nanny the goat gave her three thimblefuls of milk every day and was no expense to keep.

Nanny was a sturdy creature, in spite of her years, and scrambled all

day among the rocks, getting a very good living by nibbling the scanty little bushes that clung to the crevices. In winter, when there were no leaves on the bushes, she browsed on their shadows that slipped over the boulders. And the old lady always saved for her half of the kitchen scraps. Every evening, the little old lady would hear Nanny's little old cracked bell clambering up the mountainside, and then she would go out with the kitchen scraps, and the goat would give her the three thimblefuls of milk in return. She had a very pleasant disposition—for a goat—and so the milk was very sweet and good.

Every Thursday, Hannah the hen laid one egg. On Sundays, Mondays, Tuesdays, and Wednesdays she cackled incessantly about her plans for laying it. On Fridays and Saturdays she cackled even louder

about having laid it, so that even Nanny got tired of her. However, the Thursday egg was quite a help to the little old lady, so she gave the hen the other half of the kitchen scraps and all the worms in the pocket-handkerchief garden and talked to her as little as necessary.

Even with these helps, however, the old lady had to be quite industrious to make her money last. But she was naturally spry and she had, besides, a wise old heart under her kerchief. And so, in summer and winter, she lived quite happy and content with her tea-kettle and her cricket and her tabby cat.

But one short, grey, snowy winter day the old lady felt something like clouds gathering and stirring under her bodice all morning. She bustled more than ever about her work and thought to cure her queer cloudy feeling by making three little seed-cakes, for it was the day before Christmas. The largest cake wasn't much bigger than a toadstool, but the old lady calculated that the three cakes would last her and the tabby cat and the cricket till New Year's.

About four o'clock in the afternoon she found her heart very heavy in her breast. She looked out of her window at the grey sky and at the snow that was beginning to round off the sharp corners of the rocks, and she suddenly knew that she just *had* to do something to help that queer feeling on the inside of her. She looked at the tabby cat sleeping soundly in the chimney corner, and she looked at the tea-kettle hanging over the coals. It hadn't said anything yet, for she had just put it on, so it just hung there, quite glum and unsociable.

And then she happened to see the seed-cakes that she had left to cool on the chimney-shelf. "I can spare one," she said to herself, "and there's the lame herb-gatherer's wife been sick abed, and without a crumb extry for Christmas, I dare say."

She was very glad indeed that she had thought of this, and she began to feel quite light and bright inside as she wrapped up the one seed-cake in her one linen napkin and pinned her old grey shawl about her head.

86

'PILIO

Br-r-r-r-h! The wind snatched at her as she set foot across the doorstep and filliped her cheeks and snapped her shawl about. She was a little flurried by his familiarity, but she knew that he was only a rough, playful fellow who didn't know any better, so she scurried on before him like a rabbit, chuckling as she went. She followed the nanny goat's path around the edge of the mountain and down a little way on the other side. Pretty soon she came to the herb-gatherer's hut.

She gave the cake to the sick woman, who was very glad to have it, and gladder still to see a visitor on such a grey afternoon. But soon it was time for the little old lady to go scurrying back up the path toward her little house.

At first she felt bright and warm inside from her visit, but pretty soon she realized that she was beginning to feel heavy and cold again. So she decided to look closely, as she went, for a sprig of bright berries or something pretty to take home and put on the chimney-shelf.

"It's something *extry* you seem to be wanting," she said to herself (trying to speak sharply), "because it's Christmas Eve. If you could only find a little bunch of red and yellow leaves, now, like you took in the house for Thanksgiving, perhaps you'd be more content."

But every leaf on the scant bushes had fallen; every bit of moss or lichen was covered with snow. Not a thing did she see that she could pluck and treasure.

Then, she fairly lost her breath when a redbird came flashing out of the snow-whirl and perched for a moment on a boulder beside the path. "Oh, I wish I could take you home!" she gasped.

The redbird heard her, and cast back at her a look of the utmost astonishment as he went whirring off again into the drifts. "Me?" she heard him say. And indeed his eyes were so bright and his topknot so stiff and his voice so sharp that she was very much abashed. She wondered what had ever possessed her even to dream that such a wild, gorgeous, free-winged creature might ever stir the still air in her little house.

"A hankering old body you are," she scolded herself, as she hurried up the path. "With a cricket and a tea-kettle and a tabby cat of your own for kinfolks! And a hen that lays an egg every week of the world and a milk goat for friends —!"

When she reached home she determined to keep busy. She hurried in to get the kitchen scraps and her pail. Then she went out to the nanny goat's shed and sat down on her little three-legged stool. Usually, she and the nanny goat understood each other without many words, but this evening she felt an unusual need of conversation.

"It's bitter cold," she began, for she knew she would have to do most of

88

the talking, "and the drifts will be knee-high and more by morning. Look how the snow swirls around the corner of the shed! And it's Christmas Eve, Nanny. You and I have lived together here many a long year. Time wags along pretty well, the year round. And a chimney-place and a shed of our own aren't to be sneezed at. But come Christmas, seems like a body kinda wants a little something extry."

"Well," said the goat, with her mouth full of scraps, "all's as it is."

The old lady picked up her stool. She had finished milking by this time. She told herself that she should know better than to look for sociable conversation from the nanny goat.

Still feeling unsettled and heavy-hearted, she took the rest of the kitchen scraps to the henhouse for Hannah. Hannah was already asleep on her perch, round as a ball, with every feather sticking out a different way. The minute she heard the old lady at the door, however, she jumped up and stretched out her neck excitedly.

"Last Thursday week I says to Nanny," she began, talking very fast and at the top of her voice, "you'll find the egg over there behind the

feed box—about the biggest one I've laid since the day I found the big worm under the cabbage leaf. Law sakes! says I, I never seen the worms so skinny and scarce as they is this year since the big hawk flew over the henhouse an' —"

The little old lady shut the henhouse door on her cackling and fled.

The wind went racing after her to her very doorstep, but she pattered in and shut the door in his face. The kettle was singing busily now, and the tabby cat was purring, and the cricket was tuning up. The fire shone on the polished stomach of the kettle, and altogether the little house seemed very warm and bright. Beyond the windows the snow dropped a soft, grey curtain, and the wind whistling down the chimney made it seem all the cozier within. The old lady drew her little old chair up to the fire and put her slippers on the fender. She began to tell herself again that she was a wicked old body to be wishful and discontented and to fly into a temper on Christmas Eve.

And then, even as she was scolding herself, she began to feel heavier and colder inside than ever. "I know what I'll do," she said at last, jumping up from her place. "Since I couldn't find any leaves or berries, I'll go get the branches I brought in Thanksgiving, and set them on the chimney-piece, and watch the fire dance on the two red leaves that are left. That will be a little something extry."

So she bustled over to the window seat, where, ever since she had brought them in to decorate the house for Thanksgiving, she had kept the branch of leaves in a jug of water. It was the sunniest window she had, and she liked to sit there and darn her stockings on bright afternoons, and she could look up over her spectacles now and then and see the sun shining on the red and yellow leaves. But they had been in the warm room over a month, now, and one by one all the bright leaves had dropped off, except two.

The little old lady lifted the jug that held the bare branches and the two leaves and took it over to the fire and set it on the chimney-piece.

90

Then she sat down again in her little chair beside the tabby cat and folded her hands in her lap and settled herself to make the most of what she had.

It was very still in the little room. Except for the sleepy purring of the tea kettle and the cat there was not a sound. And except for the dancing of the flames and shadows, there was not a motion. Once the old lady, gazing so steadily at the two red leaves, nodded. Then snapping her eyes open, she thought she saw something that had not been there before on the bare twig between them. She thought it must be a bit of dry bark at first. Then she saw that it was a small creature hanging upside down by six slender legs, and that he had tiny bunches of wings, all satin and gold and velvet. By this time, quite breathless, she had left her chair and was standing tiptoe by the chimney-piece. She saw that the creature was moving his butterfly wings slowly and regularly, like breathing, and that as his wings grew larger his queer body grew smaller, as if all that gorgeousness were somehow being pumped out of him. Moreover, he had a quaint little face, as comical as his wings were lovely, and a long tongue, coiled up like a watch-spring. With it all, he looked very wise and mischievous, as if he had a secret which the old lady ought to be clever enough to guess.

But as for the little old lady, she was so filled with delight that she could not hold another wonder. There, on the twig, hung the empty brown chrysalis, looking for all the world like the bit of bark she had taken it to be. And to think that she had had this miracle in her warm little house for weeks! And that the butterfly should have come out and spread its wings for her on Christmas Eve, just when she was trying so hard not to long for something splendid and unusual! Why, he was as brilliant as the redbird, and ever so much gentler and more friendly. And that little brownie-like face was just the sort to hearten a body and make her chuckle on a Christmas Eve! By that time the butterfly's wings were all spread, and they were as black and velvety as midnight,

92

streaked with yellow like gold. Moreover, at last he slowly let go of the empty chrysalis, and began to flutter daintily about the room.

"Oh, look!" cried the little old lady, softly. And "Oh, look!" she cried to the tea-kettle. "Look at our fairy visitor! And look, Tabby! Did you ever see anything so lovely?"

"Uh-hm-m-m-m," answered the tea-kettle, sleepily, without so much as lifting her lid.

Tabby, however, opened one eye. "Very pur-r-r-r-ty," she murmured, and immediately went back to sleep.

But the cricket was more responsive. He hopped clear out on the hearth and stood watching the butterfly, blinking a little as he tried to follow its movements. "We used to live neighbor to a family of them," he said, not without a shade of envy in his tone. "They're all good looking— but not very steady. And not a particle of musical talent. However," he added, growing interested in spite of himself, "I used to know a butter-fly dance. It goes like this. There—join in, if you want to. I won't tell anybody."

Would you have supposed that the little old lady knew the butterfly dance? Well, she did! You've seen it, I know, of a June morning, when the yellow butterflies were dancing in pairs over the clover field, and I suppose she remembered it from the time when she was about your age.

Anyhow, it was the wildest, daintiest, strangest sight—to see the little old lady and the butterfly dancing all over the warm little, bright little house to the cricket's music on Christmas Eve! It seemed there would be no end to it—to the whirling and bowing and circling and floating. But at last it did end, and the little old lady sank down laughing into her little low chair, and the butterfly lit on her dress.

After she had rested a while, she went to her pantry and got three grains of brown sugar, which she mixed with one drop of water, and this she brought to the butterfly on the tip of her finger. He uncoiled his long watch-spring tongue and sipped it. Then he hung himself up by his heels from one of the red leaves and went fast asleep.

Well, all that winter the butterfly lived with the old lady and her relatives and kept them company. On the greyest day he was like sunshine in the house, and on the snowiest ones like summer. Along about February, one of the leaves on the branch dropped off, and a week later the other one. Then the old lady got out a bit of scarlet ribbon she had worn to the fair when she was a girl and tied it on the twig in the shape of a flower and set it in the sunniest window. And the butterfly took it for his own. And every day the old lady fed him brown sugar syrup from her finger.

But, by and by, as the winter's ice melted and the water began to drip off the eaves in the sun, the old lady began to be a little troubled. She feared that when the spring came, with the bluets and Johnny-jump-ups, the butterfly would leave her. Of course, it would be possible to keep the doors and windows shut, and so keep him imprisoned. But the more the air and the ground smelled like spring, the more she felt she could not do it. She would have to give him a chance to fly. But how she hoped that he wouldn't!

She kept him two days after the mustard bloomed in the garden, hoping. Then, when the butterfly was resting, fanning the scarlet ribbon winter-flower with his wings, she opened the window. And without so much as looking back, he drifted right out into the sunshine.

Well, for a minute the little old lady couldn't help feeling sad, but she couldn't feel sad long in such weather. Besides, from the time she opened her window, the butterflies seemed fairly swarming in her garden. Never in all her life had she had so many to look at. She had a poppy bush there, at the end of a row of cabbages, and three marigolds,

94

and a whole row of pinks. Besides, the onions bloomed, and the potatoes and the peas. As she worked in her garden the butterflies played around the little old lady like happy children. So, what with the bees and the birds to watch and Hannah and the nanny goat to attend to morning and evening, and the tabby cat sunning herself companionably on the doorstep, there was no chance to get lonesome the whole summer long.

But along in September there came a storm in the night. The next afternoon as she was gathering greens in her garden, she saw a flock of geese going over. And then the old lady began to think of the long, cold months ahead. There were times when she almost wished the butterfly had not come out on her chimney-piece, for how was she to help expecting some other such miracle now? And, after all, she had got along very well before, with her cheerful, humdrum friends and relatives.

But none of her wishing kept winter from coming. The frost fell on the garden, and the marigolds turned brown. One afternoon at tea-time, when she was sitting down alone to her tea and bread, the wind was so sharp that she decided she would have to close the door. It was bright outside, and the sun was shining, but the wind was picking up little

whirlwinds of dust, wherever it could find a bit of loose earth among the rocks. And now and then it came whirling into the old lady's kitchen.

She hated to begin taking her afternoon tea with the door shut, but she got up at last to close it. In her hand she held a slice of bread that she had just cut. But just as she started to push the door to, she stopped stock-still with her hand on the knob, for there stood a boy with his foot on the bottom step and a great green jar in his arms. That is, on the outside it was green. On the inside it was yellow like daffodils, and it was full of honey. It was so heavy that he held it in both arms, and its weight bent him backwards.

The old lady looked at the boy and the boy looked at the old lady, and then he said, "I thought you might like to have some honey on your bread."

The old lady didn't know what to say. She knew she didn't have enough money to buy honey, and she wasn't sure whether the boy meant to give it or sell it. So at last she said, "Well, maybe you'd like to have some bread with your honey?" And she held the door open so that he could see the loaf on the table.

At that the boy laughed and came right into the room, and set the great jar on the table, and the old lady cut him a slice of bread. And it was just that way that the little old lady and boy got acquainted.

97

'PILIO

He had been there almost a week before she even asked him his name. Of course she had wondered and wondered from the first, for he was as merry as a prince's son and as full of mischief and kindness. His clothes were of black velvet and satin that was yellow like marigold petals, and they were most curiously striped and embroidered. But his turned-up shoes were patched and tattered, and he was powdered all over with yellow dust, even to his cap and his curly black hair. His coat was frayed out in the back into two little tails that waved in the air when he ran, as if he were flying. Altogether, the little old lady could hardly make a guess as to where he came from. At last she asked him his name.

He looked up at her as if he knew a secret she should be clever enough to guess. "Papilio," he told her. "But they commonly call me 'Pilio."

That winter the old lady grew young again, with 'Pilio and his pranks to think of. He played hide-and-seek with the tabby cat and tweaked the lid off the tea-kettle and danced to the cricket's music, and followed the old nanny goat up and down the mountain.

Nobody ever minded his teasing except Hannah, who didn't like him at all. He was fond of dancing around the little old lady and giving her a kiss on the ear. And, if it must be confessed that he didn't do much work, at least he was always gentle and merry, and he was always spreading her bread for her out of the honey jar he had brought her.

As for the little old lady, she was always trying to mend his clothes for him and brush the dust out of his hair. But no matter how neat and mended he was in the morning, by evening his velvet coat was always frazzled out into two little tails, and the golden dust was shining in his curly hair. And at last she grew to take him just as he was, without trying to brush and mend him.

One spring day a jonquil bloomed beside the path to the shed. When 'Pilio saw it, he turned a somersault in the path, and then, slipping into the house, he peeped into the honey jar. It was almost empty. And the

98

next morning, when the little old lady got up, both 'Pilio and the jar were gone.

I wouldn't like to tell you how much the little old lady missed him that summer, and how she grieved to herself for fear he wouldn't come back. But along in September there was a storm in the night, and the next day a flock of ducks flew over. And a few days later, when she went to latch a door that was banging in the wind, there was 'Pilio on the doorstep, looking at her as mischievously as ever and lugging the honey jar as before. And it was full!

Well, since that day the little old lady always looks for him in the fall. There are butterflies in the garden all summer, and plenty of flowers and ever-changing clouds and their shadows to satisfy her need for something extra. And when the geese and ducks go over, it isn't long till 'Pilio comes.

And the cricket has nearly worn out a speech he makes about it. Whenever it turns cold early, and the little old lady can't help looking the least bit anxious, the cricket scrapes a little on his fiddle and says, in a superior sort of way, "Don't fidget, my dear. Time enough, yet. We'll need an extra seed-cake for Christmas Eve."

KARLE WILSON BAKER:
The Girl Who Wanted To Write

BY PAMELA LYNN PALMER

KARLE WILSON BAKER:
The Girl Who Wanted To Write

BY PAMELA LYNN PALMER

Little Rock, Arkansas, in the 1880's was a bustling town, set among rocky bluffs, forested with pines and hardwoods. Crisscrossed by railroad lines, the sprawling city of large Victorian houses set on lush, green lawns had formerly been a river port. Steamboats still came up the Arkansas River, and their low, mournful whistles could be heard all the way to the end of the trolley line, where the Wilsons lived in a rambling, two-storied house they called Rose Lawn.

Karl Wilson was born in Little Rock on October 13, 1878, and grew up there. She was named in memory of her mother's closest brother. Her mother, Kate Florence Montgomery Wilson, having found four names awkward, gave her daughter no middle name, figuring Karl would gain a third name when she married. Having a boy's name created some problems for Karl, and when she was fifteen, the silent "e" was added to make the name look more feminine. Still Karle continued to receive letters addressed to "Mr. Karle" throughout her life, and people reviewing her books sometimes mistook her for a man.

Karle's parents were both former school teachers. When her father, William Thomas Murphey Wilson ("Will" or "W. T." for short) decided to move to Little Rock, he took a job as a clerk in a grocery store. Within a few years he became co-owner of the store. Then, in partnership with his younger brother Richard Jackson ("Jack") Wilson, he started a wholesale grocery business which soon became one of the largest firms in town.

103

Karle had two half-sisters from her father's first marriage, Mary Louise and Ida Elizabeth. Mrs. Wilson thought "Mary" was too common a name and changed it to "May," and since Arkansawyers pronounced "Ida" as "Ider," Mrs. Wilson called the younger daughter "Beth." Karle's younger brother was named Benjamin Taylor Wilson, and a second brother, Donald, died when he was about two months old.

Karle was eight years old when she started public school. Until then her mother taught her at home because the school was several blocks from home. Karle was tall like her father, with brown eyes and blonde hair which later deepened to dark brown. She was self-conscious about her size as a child and idolized two petite little girls with long hair and ribbons in her class, not yet realizing that she, too, was considered pretty. Karle's hair was kept short and hair ribbons would simply not stay in so she was forever losing them. Her mother was often in poor health and did not have the strength to comb, braid, or curl long hair.

As long as she could remember, Karle had loved books and wanted to be a writer. When she was eight she wrote her first poem, "Home," hoping to publish it in the "Letter Box" page of *Harper's Young People* magazine. The poem included a tribute to the water pump which stood in the yard at Rose Lawn. Her mother, who had also wanted to be a writer, and Karle's Uncle Cad (Clarence Howard Montgomery), both encouraged her. Soon Karle was filling whole tablets with poems.

Mrs. Wilson's parents lived on a farm near Jacksonville, Arkansas, and the children took turns visiting them. Sometimes Grandpa Montgomery or one of Karle's uncles would drive the spring-board wagon into Little Rock. Other times Karle took the train to Jacksonville and was met at the station there. Karle loved to watch the trains roar in and out of the station. She liked to watch the people milling about, greeting friends and relatives, or sadly waving goodbye. Riding the train was a thrilling adventure. She sank into the plush red seat and watched the green and gold countryside rush by as the breeze blew in through the open windows. A born traveller, Karle didn't mind the smoke and soot and dust.

Grandpa Montgomery always liked to drive a team of handsome, spirited horses. Both of Karle's parents also admired fine horses and Karle inherited this love. Grandma Montgomery never trusted horses, though, and the family teased her about her fear. Grandpa Montgomery had been a Union officer during the Civil War and served as Attorney General of Arkansas during Reconstruction days. But when the Southerners regained control of the state government, John Rogers Montgomery retired to the farm rather than stay in Little Rock to take a lesser job.

Grandpa's house was built in two sections with a dogtrot between. One part contained the sitting room and bedrooms. The kitchen, dining room, and storage were in the other half. Grandma was a great cook and treated the family to pear preserves, blackberry and lemon pies, ginger snaps, and jelly cakes. There was always plenty of homemade bread and fresh milk and cream at meals. After dinner the family sat out on the porch. Wood chips soaked in kerosene and cottonseed oil made smoke to keep mosquitoes away. Uncle Cad sang songs like "Sweet Evelina" and "The Spanish Cavalier" while he strummed an old guitar or banjo. He even made himself a fiddle from a box until he could buy a real one. All the Montgomerys were musical, and Karle and her brother Ben both studied violin. Karle began lessons when she was nine or ten and played in various school and church ensembles.

While at her grandparents' farm, Karle was free to roam around as she pleased. The grownups were all busy with chores and only occasionally called her to help with gathering eggs or some other light task. Karle wandered about the yard, went to watch the animals feed, or walked to the grove where tall overcup oaks grew to play with the acorns and caps. Her favorite place on the farm was under the large basswood tree, where low-hanging branches created a cool, green shelter. Not far away stood a row of honey locusts with busy beehives. Behind them was the orchard, containing mostly apple trees. Late in the summer the blooming chamomile transformed the meadow in front of the orchard into a vast expanse of gold, stretching as far as the eye could see.

Karle's intense love for the beauty of nature did not make her want to live in the country. Although she liked to go on long walks to wild and deserted places to be alone with her thoughts, she also loved the city with all its noise and bustling crowds. As a teenager Karle was active in sports, church, and school. The kids all had ponies to ride or drive, and "wheels," or bicycles, had just become the rage. Having first learned to ride on rented ones in the city park, Karle and Ben soon got their own. Swimming and tennis were also popular sports. For each activity the girls had to have special clothes. Mrs. Wilson sewed the outfits herself when she was in good health; otherwise they hired a seamstress. The Baptist church which the Wilsons attended sponsored picnics, boat trips on the Arkansas River, and numerous other activities. Karle played in an orchestra organized by the Baptist Young People's Union, and her first two published poems appeared in the Union's paper, *The Baptist*, in the fall of 1892, shortly before her fourteenth birthday. In addition to their school work at Little Rock Academy, Karle and Beth took special classes in public speaking and "physical culture," probably a sort of good grooming and exercise course. They both won awards at speech tournaments. In 1893 the girls were lucky to be able to attend the World's Fair in St. Louis, Missouri. By then Beth was teaching and May had married two years before, so Karle and Ben were the only ones still in school.

In the fall of 1894, Mrs. Wilson decided to enroll Karle, Ben, and herself in Ouachita Baptist College at Arkadelphia, Arkansas. (The word "college" back then often referred to private secondary schools much like the "prep" schools of today.) Only a couple of weeks after they left for Arkadelphia, a cyclone hit Little Rock. Several people were killed and a number of businesses were demolished. Beth was visiting some friends at the time, and the whole east half of the house was blown away, but no one was badly hurt. Mr. Wilson's business was only slightly damaged. But Mrs. Wilson was upset, and also worried because her parents and husband were having money problems. She decided to return to Little Rock with Ben, but left Karle to finish the year at Ouachita Baptist College.

On her own for the first time, Karle had a grand time in Arkadelphia. At home, her mother had always carefully screened the books Karle read, allowing her to read only a few novels she approved of, and then for no more than thirty minutes a day. Free at last to read what she wished, Karle read until her eyes became strained. A letter to her mother written while she was at Ouachita showed Karle busy with orchestra rehearsals, speech tournaments, writing for the school paper, and (of course) boys. The February 1895 *Ouachita Ripples* contained Karle's essay, "A Talk about the Weather," and listed her as on the honor roll and serving as Corresponding Secretary of the Alpha Kappa (literary) Society.

The next year Karle returned to Little Rock Academy, and she continued there until she graduated in May, 1898. During her last semester she taught some classes while the school's director, Professor W. H. Tharp, went to Bristol, Virginia, to arrange to take over Southwest Virginia Institute there. Professor Tharp offered Karle a position teaching French and English at the Institute, which was then a girl's school, to begin the following fall. Karle and Beth attended classes at the University of Chicago that summer.

Meanwhile, their father's wholesale grocery business had collapsed during the Panic of 1897. While Karle was teaching in Bristol and taking coursework at the University of Chicago during the summers, her father was working for one of his brothers in San Antonio, Texas, and saving to start a new business. On a train trip, probably on his way back to Little Rock, Mr. Wilson stopped for the night in Nacogdoches, Texas. In the beautiful moonlit night, the little town nestled among large pines and rolling hills looked pretty to Mr. Wilson as he rode in a horse cab from the depot to the hotel. It had rained heavily the day before, and the driver said they would have to go around by the lower ford to cross one of the two creeks which ran through town. Mr. Wilson was tickled by the idea of settling in a place with nothing better than foot bridges across the creeks. When morning came, he liked the little town so much that he decided to start a business there. Nacogdoches was linked by railroads to a number of major cities, and within a few years, Mr. Wilson had built a wholesale grain business spanning several states.

With her savings from teaching plus some help from her parents, Karle was able to attend the University of Chicago for the whole year, from the summer of 1900 to August, 1901. Two of Karle's professors at the university were writers: Robert Herrick was a novelist who specialized in stories about women with careers; poet-dramatist William Vaughn Moody's play *The Great Divide* became a major box office success in America in 1906. Karle helped grade papers for Mr. Herrick and Mr. Moody kept promising to give her work but seemed to forget. Karle also fell in love while in Chicago, but when her boyfriend became too possessive, Karle broke up with him. Knowing her mother's health was uncertain, Karle decided to join her parents in Nacogdoches. More important, she wanted to pursue her real ambition and get some writing done.

Karle probably worked mostly on poetry during her first year in Nacogdoches. The Wilson's house burned down during Christmas week of 1902, and when Karle started a new diary a few months later, she mentioned having lost her first three journals, all her college themes, and some rejection slips she valued for personal notes from some magazine editors. Karle had managed to save most of her poems and two long short stories from the flames.

While in Nacogdoches Karle joined the Symphony Club, a woman's study group, and participated in local talent shows. Her father's success in business helped the family gain entrance into Nacogdoches society. Beth came down from Little Rock long enough to be married at her parent's home in September, 1902, but returned to Arkansas to live since her husband, Maurice Wright, was from there.

During the summer of 1903, Karle went with Beth and Maurice to Colorado Springs. There she was able to work for several hours a day at her writing, and managed to finish four short stories and several poems. Apparently she could not work as well at home because her mother wanted Karle to keep her company. Karle was becoming restless living at home and wanted to be independent of her parents. Mrs. Wilson was feeling better and the family could afford hired help for her, so Karle decided to return to Little Rock. She taught at Peabody High School for two years, returning to Nacogdoches during the summers, and continued to work on her writings. In June, 1903, *Harper's Magazine* accepted her poem "The Poet," paying $15, and printed it in the October issue. *Harper's* bought the next three poems she sold, publishing them in January, May, and October, 1905. She placed an essay and poems in several other magazines in 1905. For these early works she used the pen name "Charlotte Wilson."

By 1906 Karle was beginning to sell short stories. That summer she was able to spend a couple of months at Port Bolivar, Texas, on Galveston Island, and used the time to work on stories. Karle was then twenty-seven, and as she watched other young vacationers enjoying themselves at the beach and dances, she began to feel lonely. In an entry in her journal, written the day after her twenty-eighth birthday, she regretted her youthful claims that she would never marry and feared she might become an old maid. But less than a year passed before she married Thomas Ellis Baker.

Mr. Baker was a native of Nacogdoches County, and his family had lived there since before the Civil War. Karle had met him frequently over the years at meetings of various kinds and parties. They shared interests in music, nature, books, and civic improvements, and both had campaigned to move East Texas Baptist College from Rusk to Nacogdoches in 1902, though that attempt failed. Having known each other for years as friends, they gradually fell in love. At the time of their marriage, Mr. Baker, along with Sam Stripling and R. W. Hazelwood, was operating a drugstore on Main Street. The store had burned, along with the office of the W. T. Wilson Grain Company, in the big fire of December 23, 1906, but both businesses had recovered strongly. The new Stripling, Hazelwood, and Company store included hardware, jewelry, phonographs and records, newspapers and magazines, and a soda fountain. A director of Commercial National Bank, Mr. Baker became a vice-president of the bank a few years later, and eventually, president. Karle and Mr. Baker were married on August 8, 1907, at her parents' home on Mound Street. Their honeymoon trip included the Jamestown Exposition in Virginia, honoring the 300th anniversary of the founding of the settlement, and the traditional Niagara Falls visit.

Karle had hoped to help support her family with earnings from her writings, and since she had sold a number of short stories to major magazines including *Redbook, Cosmopolitan,* and *Century* before her marriage, her ambition was not far-fetched. One story, "The Accidental Saint," sold to *Collier's,* had brought $300. But being a wife and mother took more energy than she had expected. The Bakers' first child, Thomas Wilson ("Tomby") Baker, was born on December 1, 1908, and their daughter, Charlotte, on August 31, 1910. While the children were young Karle could not get much

109

writing done. But as they grew older, Karle managed to find time to write poems and short articles for women's magazines.

Karle wrote about family experiences—camping, making up a game to teach the children geography, balancing the household budget, and travelling the sand road by automobile. She wrote about her hobbies—photography and raising butterflies from caterpillars. What had begun as an experiment for the children turned out to be a money-making venture as Karle sold moths and butterflies, and their eggs and caterpillars, through mail order to collectors throughout the United States. Some of her neighbors thought her odd to be raising "bugs" instead of chickens. In those days, if a woman wanted to earn money, she would sell butter or eggs or sew clothes. Besides, many men thought it an insult to their ability to provide for their family if their wives tried to make money. Mr. Baker was at first embarrassed by his wife's efforts, but after she began to publish books and became well-known as a writer, he accepted her ambitions and encouraged her to continue.

As she read stories to Tomby and Charlotte, Karle became interested in writing for children. Karle wrote *The Garden of the Plynck*, reading each new chapter to the children when they came home from school in the afternoon. She finished the book in 1918 and Yale University Press published it in 1920. Karle's first two books of poems, *Blue Smoke* and *Burning Bush*, as well as her prose tales, *Old Coins*, were also published by Yale between 1919 and 1923. Karle worked on other stories for children during these years, including at least two found today in *The Reindeer's Shoe and Other Stories*. In a letter written about March, 1920, to Yale University Press, she mentioned having just finished "The Storm King's Plume" and "Pilio." "The Reindeer's Shoe" may have been written much later, for Karle read it to some children at the Houston Public Library on November 26, 1930.

Having published four books as well as poems, stories, and essays in many magazines, Karle became locally famous as an author and was frequently asked to talk at high schools, colleges, women's clubs, and literary societies all over Texas and even as far away as Boston, Massachusetts. When Stephen F. Austin State Teachers College (later University) opened in Nacogdoches in 1923, Karle was called upon to write the lyrics for the first school song, "The

Pine Tree Hymn." The next summer she taught a summer school class in contemporary poetry, then remained on the faculty for the next ten years, except for one year, 1926-1927, which she spent attending the University of California at Berkeley. Although she did not complete a college degree, Karle received an honorary Doctor of Letters from Southern Methodist University in 1924.

Karle was admired and loved as a college teacher, but found it hard to steal enough time for her writing during those years. She did write two readers for children: *Texas Flag Primer*, published in 1925 by the World Book Company and accepted as a textbook for Texas public schools, and *Two Little Texans,* also printed by the World Book Company in 1932. Southwest Press in Dallas published Karle's essays on birds, *The Birds of Tanglewood,* in 1930, as well as *Dreamers on Horseback (Collected Verse)* in 1931. *Dreamers on Horseback* was nominated for the Pulitzer Prize in Poetry.

In 1930, Karle watched the Joiner oil well come in, opening the East Texas Oil Field some 50 miles north of Nacogdoches. Anyone lucky enough to own or lease land found to contain oil could suddenly become fabulously wealthy. Incidents happening around the oil field inspired Karle's novel, *Family Style,* published by Coward-McCann in 1937. The Texas Centennial celebration sparked Karle's interest in the Texas Revolution. *Star of the Wilderness,* based on the story of Dr. James Grant's role in Texas history, was brought out by Coward-McCann in 1942. Karle's first novel, about a homemaker turned interior designer, and her last novel, about the Magee-Gutierrez revolution in Texas against Spain in 1812-1813, were never printed. The novel she and her mother worked on together, based upon Mrs. Wilson's experiences as the daughter of a Union officer during the Civil War and Reconstruction, was also never published. Still, Karle had achieved her lifetime ambition of becoming a nationally-recognized writer. She had managed to break through the barriers of the Eastern publishing world at a time when few writers, especially women, who lived west of Chicago could catch the editor's attention.

By the time Karle finished writing her last book she was about sixty-nine years old and her health was beginning to fail. Her son had succeeded his father as president of Commercial National Bank, and her daughter was publishing novels and children's books which she illustrated herself. Karle died in Nacogdoches on November 8, 1960, at the age of eighty-two.

Karle Wilson Baker loved young people and many of her stories showed young persons, especially women, striving against obstacles to fulfill their life dreams. It was not easy being a writer in a small town in Texas at a time when women were not expected to be anything more than wives and mothers. But she believed that all people, no matter how humble, had a deep need for beauty. A piece of lace or ribbon on a farm woman's dress, flowers planted in an old lard can beside a tenant farm shack—these were human expressions of that yearning. And Karle hoped, through her writings, to capture and preserve the beauty of such simple things for those who could not express this need in words, or art, or song.

For additional information on Karle Wilson Baker, see:

Gaston, Edwin W., Jr., "Karle Wilson Baker: First Woman of Texas Letters," *East Texas Historical Journal,* XV (Fall, 1977) 45-51.

Palmer, Pamela Lynn, "Karle Wilson Baker and the East Texas Experience," *East Texas Historical Journal*, XXIV (Fall, 1986) 46-58.

Palmer, Pamela Lynn, "Dorothy Scarborough and Karle Wilson Baker: A Literary Friendship," *Southwestern Historical Quarterly*, XCI (July, 1987) 19-32.

Karle Wilson Baker Papers, Special Collections, Ralph W., Steen Library, Stephen F. Austin State University, Nacogdoches, Texas.